ZOOM

A wheelie good book of colours!

PANDA

Zebra drives a dumper truck so big and bright and blue.

"I'll win the race! I'm in first place! There's nothing you can do!"

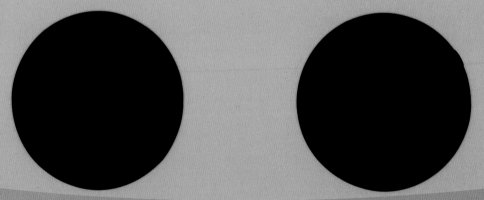

"Not so fast!" cries Elephant.
"Look who's number one!
Without a fuss, my big red bus
is winning – oh, what fun!"

Monkey then comes zooming by
and gives a smart salute.
"My yellow digger's in the lead.
You won't catch me!"

TOOT TOOT!

"Tee-hee!" laughs cuddly Panda
in her orange racing car.

"I am the best, forget the rest –
I'm a racing superstar!"

Then a bright green bulldozer comes rumbling, tumbling past.

Bouncy **Bear** leaps in the air –

"I am so super-fast!"

With a sparkly sheen, **black** limousine now leads this racing pack!

Toucan drives his mean machine –
his friends sit in the back.

Look out! A **purple** motorbike
pulls an overtaking stunt!

Warthog shouts,
"You're all too slow!"
as he races to the front.

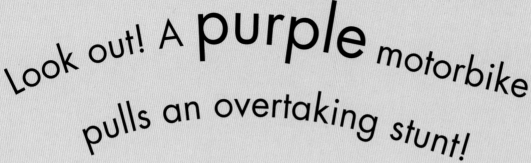

Parrot squawks to everyone,
"I'm the **fastest** kid in town!"

Her motorhome is in first place –

it's painted chocolate **brown**.

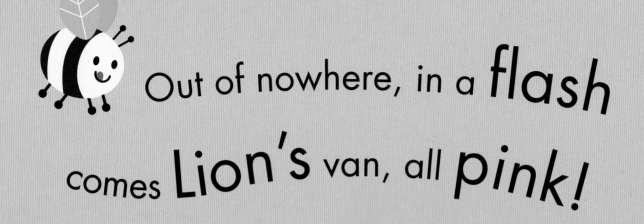

Out of nowhere, in a **flash** comes **Lion's** van, all **pink!**

"Enjoy your race for **second** place," he shouts, and gives a wink!

As roaring **Lion** nears the end,
he stops to give a bow.

That may be a **big** mistake –
whose car will **win** it now?

Nobody can believe it,
when in a sudden burst,

Tortoise in his **rainbow** car
zooms from last to **first!**